Silly & Sillier

Silly

Sillier

Read-Aloud Tales *from* Around *the* World

Told by Judy Sierra
Illustrated by Valeri Gorbachev

ALFRED A. KNOPF
New York

For Max
—J.S.

For Isabel Warren-Lynch and Janet Schulman
—V.G.

THIS IS A BORZOI BOOK PUBLISHED BY ALFRED A. KNOPF

Text copyright © 2002 by Judy Sierra
Illustrations copyright © 2002 by Valeri Gorbachev

"The Teeny-Tiny Chick and the Sneaky Old Cat" adapted from "The Little Chicken and the Old Cat,"
which appeared in *Burmese Folk-Tales* by Maung Htin Aung.
Reproduced by permission of Oxford University Press, New Delhi, India.

"Why Do Monkeys Live in Trees?" first appeared in a slightly different form in *Multicultural Folktales* by Judy Sierra
and Bob Kaminski. Reproduced by permission of Oryx Press, Westport, Connecticut.

www.randomhouse.com/kids

Library of Congress Cataloging-in-Publication Data
Sierra, Judy.
Silly and sillier : read-aloud tales from around the world / told by Judy Sierra ; illustrated by Valeri Gorbachev.
p.   cm.
Includes bibliographical references.
Summary: A compilation of folktales from twenty different cultures,
each of which contains elements suited to storytelling for young children.
ISBN 0-375-80609-1 (trade) — ISBN 0-375-90609-6 (lib. bdg.)
1. Tales. [1. Folklore. 2. Storytelling—Collections.] I. Gorbachev, Valeri, ill. II. Title.
PZ8.1.S573 Si 2002
398.2—dc21
[E]   00-048133

Printed in the United States of America
September 2002

10 9 8 7 6 5 4 3 2 1
First Edition

CONTENTS

A Note to Parents and All Storytellers

Silly and Sillier (England)   1

Toontoony Bird (Bangladesh)   4

Clever Mandy (Bahamas)   8

Magical Mice (Japan)   14

The Coyote and the Lizard (United States: Pueblo Indian)   18

Bear Squash-You-All-Flat (Russia)   22

The Koala and the Kangaroo (Australia: Aborigine)   26

Jabuti and Jaguar Go Courting (Brazil)   30

Why Do Monkeys Live in Trees? (Ghana)   35

Juan Bobo (Argentina)   39

The Wonderful Pancake (Ireland)   43

Kuratko the Terrible (Czech Republic)   47

Too Many Fish (Borneo)   51

The Tortoise and the Iroko Man (Nigeria)   55

Don't Wake King Alimango (Philippines)   59

Buggy Wuggy (Italy)   63

The Teeny-Tiny Chick and the Sneaky Old Cat
(Myanmar, formerly Burma)   67

The Singing Pumpkin (Iran)   70

The Mighty Caterpillar (South Africa: Masai)   74

One Good Turn Deserves Another (Mexico)   79

Bibliography   84

About the Author and Illustrator   86

A NOTE TO PARENTS
AND ALL STORYTELLERS

Here is a collection of the world's funniest stories to read aloud to children ages three to seven. These traditional tales, ones that have been passed down by word of mouth from generation to generation, come from twenty countries and six continents. For at least as long as people have kept written records, we know that parents and grandparents have told children stories about talking animals, magic, and monsters. Nowadays, teachers and librarians join family members in recounting these sorts of tales to children.

What tickles a young child's funny bone? Repetition, in and of itself, can be hilarious to children. Talking objects, like the stick and the fire in "Toontoony Bird," a tale from Bangladesh, provoke giggles. And so do unusual-sounding nonsense words, like the name of the witch, Koolimasunder W. Diamondpaw, in "Clever Mandy," a tale from the Bahamas. When these words and names and phrases are repeated for the second or third time, children will delight in saying them right along with you.

But these seemingly silly tales are also offering important lessons. Good is rewarded and wrongdoing is punished. The smallest and least significant creatures prove to be the most helpful friends—or the most fearsome enemies. Cleverness and trickery are important tools of the small and weak, but they must never be used thoughtlessly. The lowly tortoise in the Nigerian tale "The Tortoise and the Iroko Man," who tricks innocent bystanders into taking his punishment, is himself punished by having his smooth shell cracked for all eternity. These tales reinforce a child's strong sense of justice while providing a glimpse into other lands and cultures.

In most of the tales in this collection, the weakest animal or the smallest child triumphs through cleverness, kindness, and persistence. And, probably because grandparents and other elders were frequently the family's storytellers, some of the stories have old men and old women as the heroes and heroines.

Children love to hear accounts of powerful adults, terrible monsters, and dangerous animals who behave like complete idiots. Stories reveal harmless fools for what they are, but evil fools are punished, or tricked into punishing themselves, like the giant who begs the tiny mouse deer to tie him up in "Too Many Fish," a tale from Borneo.

Part of the fun of sharing stories from far-flung regions of the world is discovering the ways in which they are similar to favorite stories we've long known. I've included a tale from the Bahamas that resembles "Rumpelstiltskin." In it Clever Mandy must guess the name of a witch or be her servant forever. A Czech rooster named Kuratko the Terrible devours a series of bigger and bigger people, objects, and animals, much like the infamous old lady who swallowed a fly. The Irish tale "The Wonderful Pancake" begins like "The Little Red Hen," but when the hen and her lazy housemates start to argue over who will eat the pancake, the little pancake jumps out of the pan, runs away, and has an adventure like that of the Gingerbread Man.

Storytellers in many cultures use short, formulaic beginnings and endings for their tales, like our "once upon a time." I have included these with stories whenever possible. The beginning formula lets listeners know that the story that follows, though true on one level, is make-believe. The Irish tale "The Wonderful Pancake" happened "once upon a time, when pigs were swine and birds made their nests in old men's beards." The opening formula, *yaki boud, yaki na boud* (once there was and once there was not), used in "The Singing Pumpkin," our Iranian tale, conveys perfectly the idea that stories are both true and untrue. Ending formulas return the listener to the real world, sometimes by passing the role of storyteller to the next person, as in the Argentine

> *"Zapatito roto, y usted me cuenta otro.*
> Little broken shoe, the next tale comes from *you*."

Zestful dramatization will make these stories even more fun for young listeners. There are rhymes and chants that want to be sung. There are gullible giants, sneaky tricksters, annoying bugs, pompous kings, and small heroes and heroines who beg that you portray them with booming voices, squeaky voices, or just plain silly voices. The words and chants in the stories are often onomatopoeic, more sound than sense, and defy translation. I have left many in the original language. You and your listeners can invent your own pronunciations for these foreign words and your own melodies for the rhymes, chants, and jingles. In doing so, you will make these tales truly your own. Enjoy!

—Judy Sierra
September 2002

SILLY AND SILLIER
England

Jack was born to a family of noodleheads, numskulls, and ninnyhammers. So when his father decided to build a house, Jack was worried. Still, it turned out to be a good, solid house. It was perfect, in fact, except for one thing.

"It's too dark inside," said Jack's father. "Fetch a bucket, son, and help me haul sunlight into the house." Jack and his father ran in and out, dumping buckets full of sunlight on the floor, but the house was just as dark as before.

"You know, Dad," said Jack, "if you make some windows, they'll let in the sunlight."

"Why didn't you say so?" said Jack's father. He grabbed a saw and cut windows in all the walls. Then he and Jack went to buy glass to put in their new windows and left the saw lying on the ground. When Jack and his father came home, they found Jack's mother crying her eyes out.

"Look at that saw there on the ground," Jack's mother sobbed. "Suppose our Jack gets married and has a baby, and the baby crawls along and cuts himself on that saw!"

Jack's brother, Tom, jumped up. "I'll punish that saw right now!" he shouted. "I'll drown that saw before it can hurt Jack's poor little baby."

Jack watched his brother pick up the saw, carry it to the river, and drop it in the water. He shook his head in disbelief. "You threw away a perfectly good saw," said Jack. "I don't think anyone in the world is as silly as my family. I am leaving, and I won't come back until I meet three bigger sillies than you."

Jack put on his coat, his hat, and his boots, and set off down the road. Around sunset, he knocked at the door of an inn and asked for a room.

"Would you like something to eat before you go to bed?" the innkeeper asked.

"I'll have a hard-boiled egg," Jack answered.

Soon the most horrible sounds came from the kitchen. *Squawk-awk-awk!* Jack ran to see what was happening. There was the innkeeper, holding a pot of boiling water in one hand and a hen in the other. *Squawk-awk-awk!* shrieked the hen. The innkeeper shook his head. "How can I make you a hard-boiled egg," he asked, "when my hen won't drink this boiling water?"

So Jack had to teach the innkeeper how to take an egg and cook it in a pan of boiling water.

"That's one silly," said Jack, and he went to his room and lay down on the bed.

He tried to sleep, but he couldn't because he was so cold, and that was because the blanket only came up to his waist. When he pulled it up under his chin, his feet stuck out at the bottom.

Jack called the maid and said, "Please bring me a longer blanket."

"No, no," said the maid. "I'll just make this one longer." She cut a strip off the bottom of the blanket, then sewed that strip to the top of the blanket. "It's longer now," she said.

"You," said Jack, "are silly number two."

Early the next morning, a loud noise rattled the ceiling above Jack's bed. *Thump, thump, thump—wham! Thump, thump, thump—wham!* He rushed upstairs to see what was the matter. He couldn't believe his eyes. A man had hooked the top of his trousers over two chairs. He ran across the room, *thump, thump, thump,* and tried to jump into the trousers, but every time he jumped, he landed flat on the floor, *wham!*

Jack had to teach the man how to sit on the edge of the bed and put his legs into his pants one at a time. "So that's how you do it!" said the man, and he thanked Jack for his help.

"That makes three sillies," said Jack, and he went back home, as he said he would. I heard that Jack and Tom opened a shop, and they're doing very well for themselves selling used ice cream cones, square bowling balls, and fireproof matches to all the other sillies in their town.

TOONTOONY BIRD
Bangladesh

In the eggplant garden, Toontoony the Tailor Bird danced and sang, *toon-toon-a-toon-toon, da-eeee!* Toontoony wasn't watching where he was dancing. He stepped on a thorn, and the thorn stuck in his foot—*oof!* That hurt! Off he hopped to the barbershop and begged, "Barber, please, sir, get your tweezers. Pull this thorn out of my foot."

"Harrumph!" the barber huffed. "I'm the royal barber. I shave His Majesty the Raja. Never will I touch the foot of a bird."

Toontoony hopped to the Raja's palace, where he found the Raja sitting in his royal tub. "Your Majesty, please make the barber pull this thorn out of my foot."

The Raja looked at Toontoony and laughed, "Ha, ha, ha," until his belly shook. "Why should I do that for you? Who do you think you are? Ha, ha, ha."

Toontoony hopped through the Raja's house until he came to a mouse hole. He tapped his beak on the wall, *tap, tap*.

"Come in," said the mouse.

"Dear mouse," said the bird, "be a good friend. Run and bite the Raja's belly."

"No!" squeaked the mouse. "I don't dare bite the Raja's royal belly."

Toontoony hopped to the courtyard, where a cat lay napping in the sun. "Dear cat," said Toontoony, "please chase the mouse."

"Some other time," the cat yawned. "Can't you see I'm busy?"

Toontoony hopped to the road and he found a stick. "Dear stick," said Toontoony, "won't you swat the cat?"

"I wouldn't do that. I'm a friend of the cat's," the stick told Toontoony.

Toontoony hopped and hopped and he came to a fire. "Dear fire," said Toontoony, "come along quick and burn the stick."

"I'm too hot to be bothered," sputtered the fire.

Toontoony hopped and hopped and he came to the ocean. "Dear ocean," said the bird, "please rise higher and put out the fire."

"That's absurd—taking orders from a bird!" scoffed the ocean.

Toontoony hopped and hopped and he met an elephant. "Dear elephant," said the bird, "please drink the ocean."

"Drink the ocean? What a silly notion."

Toontoony's foot hurt so much, and he was so tired of hopping. He sat down on the ground and began to cry. A mosquito flew down, landed next to him, and asked, "What's the matter, Cousin Toontoony?"

"I have a thorn in my foot," said the bird. "And it hurts, and the royal barber won't pull it out, and the Raja won't punish the barber, and the mouse won't bite the Raja's big laughing belly, and the cat won't chase the mouse, and the stick won't swat the cat, and the fire won't burn the stick, and the ocean won't put out the fire, and the elephant won't drink the ocean."

"I could bite the elephant," said the mosquito.

"An elephant wouldn't feel a mosquito bite," said Toontoony.

"He might," said the mosquito, and she disappeared. Soon the sky darkened. Millions of mosquitoes flew in a swarm toward the elephant, all of them buzzing, "You'd better do what Toontoony says! You'd better do what Toontoony says!"

Right away, the elephant began to drink the ocean. The ocean began to put out the fire. The fire began to burn the stick. The stick began to swat the cat. The cat began to chase the mouse. The mouse began to bite the Raja's big laughing belly.

"Barber! Barber!" the Raja shouted. "Pull the thorn out of Toontoony's foot right now!"

The royal barber pulled the thorn, and once again Toontoony danced in the eggplant garden and sang, *toon-toon-a-toon-toon, da-eeee!*

CLEVER MANDY
Bahamas

Once upon a time, in the old people's time, when the monkey chewed tobacco and spit white lime, a girl named Mandy left home to seek her fortune. Mandy didn't know where her fortune might be, so she walked and walked. She met an old woman, and the old woman asked, "Where you goin', me girl?"

"I don't know where, ma'am," Mandy answered. "I'm seeking my fortune."

"Come to my house, then," said the old woman. "If you work a year and do everything I say, I'll give you half my treasure."

So Mandy went home with the woman, and didn't she work every day from before sunrise till after sunset! When the year was up and it was time for Mandy to get her pay, the old woman said, "Well, now, Mandy, before the sun goes down today, you must guess my name. If you do, you will get half my treasure. If you don't, you will work for me forever."

Mandy was scared and she started to run. Then she remembered the gold and jewels she'd seen in the old woman's house, and she thought about how hard she had worked all year. "Who would know the old woman's name?" she asked herself.

Mandy found Sis' Cat and asked, "Kitty-katty, kitty-katty, do you know the old woman's name?"

Sis' Cat said, "Yes, I know, but I can't say so."

Mandy found Br'er Dog and asked, "Diggy-doggy, diggy-doggy, do you know the old woman's name?"

Br'er Dog said, "Yes, I know, but I can't say so."

Down by the river, Mandy found Br'er Crab. "Cribby-crabby, cribby-crabby, do you know the old woman's name?"

Br'er Crab said, "Yes, I know . . . but . . . I can't . . ."

"Can't what?" asked Mandy.

"I can't tell you that her name is Koolimasunder W. Diamondpaw. She'd be mighty mad if I told you that!"

Mandy was so glad, she skipped on back to the old woman's house.

The old woman said, "Mandy, night's comin'. Time for you to guess my name, otherwise you are mine forever."

"Can I guess three names?" asked Mandy.

"Go ahead," the old woman laughed. "Guess a hundred names, but you still won't guess *my* name."

"Is your name Aunt Sally Bunch?" asked Mandy.

"No, it ain't."

"Is your name Granny Grinny-Granny?" asked Mandy.

"Ain't that, neither."

"Then your name *must* be Koolimasunder W. Diamondpaw."

Hoo! The old woman was so surprised, she flew up in the air! She ran to Sis' Cat, grabbed her by the neck, and said, "Kitty-katty, kitty-katty, did you tell Mandy my name?"

Sis' Cat looked her in the eye. "No, no, no, I didn't say so."

The old woman went to Br'er Dog, grabbed him by the ears, and said, "Diggy-doggy, diggy-doggy, did you tell Mandy my name?"

Br'er Dog looked her right in the eye. "No, no, no, I didn't say so."

The old woman grabbed her walking stick, went to the river, and roused Br'er Crab. "Cribby-crabby, cribby-crabby," she said, "did you tell Mandy my name?"

Br'er Crab looked down and said, "No-o-o-o."

"Yes, you did!" screamed the old woman.

Br'er Crab swam toward his hole, but before he could get inside, the old woman hit him on the back with her stick, *kuludung!* Up until that instant, Br'er Crab had a soft back, but when that stick touched it, it turned into a hard shell. It's been that way ever since.

Then Mandy took a blanket and filled it with half the old woman's treasure and carried it home. And then she told everyone her story so the old woman wouldn't be able to catch a girl or a boy ever again. Now everybody knows her name is . . .

That's right! Koolimasunder W. Diamondpaw.

Ben billy ben,
This story end.

MAGICAL MICE
Japan

Mukashi, mukashi, a story, a story.

A kind old man and a kind old woman once lived on a farm, and each morning, the kind old woman made delicious cakes called *dango*. The kind old man put some *dango* into a little box that he carried with him when he went to work in the fields. One day, when the man sat down and opened the box, a *dango* dropped to the ground and rolled along, *koro, koro, koro,* and disappeared.

The old man got down on his hands and knees and looked for the *dango,* but he couldn't find it. Then he heard tiny voices singing. The sound came from a hole in the ground. The man bent down and peered inside.

Paaann! All of a sudden, the hole became very big—so big that he could put his head in it. What did he see? The magical underground kingdom of the mice! Everywhere, mice were cooking, mice were weaving, mice were painting, and mice were playing music. Mice were dancing around the *dango* and singing,

"All the cats have gone away,
Now the mice can sing and play!"

"May no cats ever disturb your beautiful kingdom," said the kind old man.
The biggest mouse looked up at him and said, "Thank you for the magnificent *dango*. In return, we would like to give you this magic hammer. When you strike it on the ground, you will have good fortune."

The kind old man thanked the mouse. Then he ran home to share the good fortune with his wife. What the mouse had said was true. Each time they struck the hammer on the ground—*pika, pika, pika*—gold coins appeared!

It wasn't long before their mean, greedy neighbor heard about their gift. He visited the kind old man and the kind old woman and asked, "What's this I hear about a magic hammer?" The kind old man told him of his adventure with the mice.

The next morning, the mean old man took his own *dango* to the field and dropped it on the ground. Away it rolled, *koro, koro, koro,* and disappeared. The mean old man searched on his hands and knees until he found the mouse hole. He bent down to look inside. *Paaann!* The mouse hole opened. The mean old man put his head inside, and what did he see? The magical underground kingdom of the mice! Everywhere, mice were cooking, mice were weaving, mice were painting, and mice were playing music. Mice were dancing around the *dango* and singing,

> "All the cats have gone away,
> Now the mice can sing and play!"

That man was so mean! He meowed like a cat, *nayaan, nayaan!* The frightened mice squeaked in fear and disappeared.

Paaann! The door to the magical mouse kingdom became small again. Unfortunately, the mean old man's head was still underground. No matter how much he pounded and punched and pushed and kicked, he couldn't get his head out of the mouse hole.

Everyone in the neighborhood gathered around and laughed for a long time. Finally, they dug the mean old man out of the dirt, and he ran home without even saying thank you. He never did get a magic hammer. As for the kind old man and the kind old woman, they lived the rest of their lives in peace and prosperity.

THE COYOTE AND THE LIZARD
United States: Pueblo Indian

Down by Laguna Pueblo, there is a big sandstone rock that overhangs the road.
A lizard once lived on the sunny side of that rock, and all day long, she sang,

"Moki, *moki, moki,*
Moki, *moki, moki,*
Hanging Rock is here,
A happy home for me."

The coyote was going along and he heard the lizard's song. Now, everything nice or pretty that someone else has, the coyote wants for himself, so he wanted that song. "I must get the lizard to teach me her song," he said, and he jumped onto the rock.

"Good morning, my friend. You are such a good singer, and your song is so pretty, I wish you would teach it to me."

"I will," said the lizard, and she sang,

"Moki, moki, moki,
Moki, moki, moki,
Hanging Rock is here,
A happy home for me."

"Thank you, my friend," said the coyote. Away he trotted, singing as he went,

"Moki, moki, moki,
Moki, moki, moki,
Hanging Rock is here,
A happy home for me."

He passed by a pond where some wild ducks were feeding. He didn't see the ducks, but they saw him. They flew up in the air, flapping their wings and quacking. The noise frightened the coyote so badly that he forgot the song. "Muki, muki, muki," he sang. "No, that's not right. Maki, maki, maki? No, no, no!"

He trotted back to Hanging Rock. "My friend," said the coyote, "I have forgotten the song you taught me. Won't you please sing it again?"

The lizard sang her song again, and the coyote ran along the road singing,

"Moki, moki, moki,
Moki, moki, moki,
Hanging Rock is here,
A happy home for me."

But he hadn't gone very far when a rabbit jumped from behind a bush and scared him so much that he forgot the song. "Poki, poki, poki," he sang. "No, that isn't it. Doki, doki, doki? No, no, no!"

The coyote turned tail and ran back to the lizard's place. He found her snoozing in the warm sunshine.

"Hey, Lizard! I forgot the song," yipped the coyote. "Teach it to me again."

The lizard did not answer.

"I will ask you three more times," the coyote growled. "Then, if you don't sing your song, I will eat you up."

The lizard kept her eyes closed and paid no attention.

"Sing me that song!"

—no answer.

"Sing me that song!"

—no answer.

"Sing me that song!"

—no answer.

The coyote opened his big mouth and swallowed the lizard in one gulp. Then he found a soft patch of pine needles, lay down, and fell asleep. While he dozed, the lizard took out her little knife. It was the kind of knife lizards use to remove their old skin each year. She cut a hole in the coyote's side and wiggled out. The lizard looked around until she found a rock just her size and popped it into the coyote's belly. She took out her sewing kit and stitched him back together with a piece of sinew thread. Then she hurried home to Hanging Rock.

All this time, believe it or not, the coyote was fast asleep. When he awoke, he trotted to the pond for a drink. "That little lizard sure is heavy," he complained. "She is hurting my insides. I wish I had never heard her silly, no-good song. How did it go?"

Back at her sunny rock, the lizard was singing,

> "*Moki, moki, moki,*
> *Moki, moki, moki,*
> Hanging Rock is here,
> A happy home for me.
> *Mmm-hmm, mmm-hmm.*"

BEAR SQUASH-YOU-ALL-FLAT
Russia

Once upon a time, a mitten lay in a meadow. Someone must have dropped it in the snow the winter before, and now it lay dry and warm in the spring sunshine.

Along came Whiskery Mouse, *pit, pat, pit,* twirling his whiskers. He looked at the mitten and saw a perfect home for a mouse. He stood in front and called out, "Little house, little house! Who lives in this little house?"

No one answered, for there was no one inside.

"I will live here myself," said Whiskery Mouse, and in he went and made a cozy home for himself.

Along came Croaker the Frog, *jump, jump, jump.* "Little house, little house! Who lives in this little house?"

"I do. Whiskery Mouse. Who are you?"

"I am Croaker the Frog. May I come inside and live with you?"

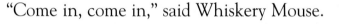

"Come in, come in," said Whiskery Mouse.

So the frog went in, and they began to live together.

Along came Hoppity Hare, *hop, hop, hop.* "Little house, little house! Who lives in this little house?"

"We do! We are Whiskery Mouse and Croaker the Frog. Who are you?"

"I am Hoppity Hare. May I come inside and live with you?"

"Come in, come in," said Whiskery Mouse and Croaker the Frog.

So the hare put his ears down and crawled in, and they began to live together.

Along came Frisky Fox, *trot, trot, trot.* "Little house, little house! Who lives in this little house?"

"We do! We are Whiskery Mouse and Croaker the Frog and Hoppity Hare. Who are you?"

"I am Frisky Fox. May I come inside and live with you?"

"Come in, come in," said Whiskery Mouse and Croaker the Frog and Hoppity Hare.

So he crawled in, and they began to live together.

Along came Sneaky Wolf, *sneak, sneak, sneak.* "Little house, little house! Who lives in this little house?"

"We do! We are Whiskery Mouse and Croaker the Frog and Hoppity Hare and Frisky Fox. Who are you?"

"I am Sneaky Wolf. May I come inside and live with you?"

"Come in, come in," said Whiskery Mouse and Croaker the Frog and Hoppity Hare and Frisky Fox.

So he crawled in, and they began to live together.

Along came Bear Squash-You-All-Flat, *squash, squash, squash.* "Little house, little house! Who lives in this little house?"

"We do! We are Whiskery Mouse and Croaker the Frog and Hoppity Hare and Frisky Fox and Sneaky Wolf. Who are you?"

"I am Bear Squash-You-All-Flat. May I come inside and live with you?"

"Come in, come in," said Whiskery Mouse and Croaker the Frog and Hoppity Hare and Frisky Fox and Sneaky Wolf.

So Bear Squash-You-All-Flat put his nose inside, and his head inside, and his two big paws inside, and—BOOM! That was the end of the little house, and Whiskery Mouse and Croaker the Frog and Hoppity Hare and Frisky Fox and Sneaky Wolf all ran away.

THE KOALA AND THE KANGAROO
Australia: Aborigine

The koala lives high in the gum tree, and he doesn't come down to drink. All the water he needs he gets by chewing the gum tree's leaves. But long ago, the koala lived on the ground with his friend the kangaroo. In those days, the koala had a splendid tail, a fluffy tail, a tail longer than he was tall. The koala

was so pleased with his tail, he spent most of his time combing it and stroking it with his claws. This is the story of how he lost that tail, and why he stays up high in the gum tree.

A drought came. Lakes and rivers dried up, and the animals were thirsty. "If it doesn't rain soon, we might die," said the koala to the kangaroo. "What should we do?"

"I've been thinking," said the kangaroo to the koala. "When I was a little joey in my mother's pouch, there was a drought. My mother went to the dry riverbed. She found a special place, and she dug a hole, and the hole filled with water."

"Could you find that special place again?" asked the koala.

"I think so," said the kangaroo. "It wasn't a place of hard, dry mud, and it wasn't a place of big, sharp rocks. It was a place of small gravel."

The two friends hurried to the dry riverbed. They hopped across the hard, dry mud, and they scrambled over the big, sharp rocks, and they came to a place of small gravel.

"Why don't you dig first," said the koala to the kangaroo.

The kangaroo began to dig with his short front legs. He dug, and he dug, and he dug, and he threw out gravel, *ka-ching, ka-ching!* He dug, and he dug,

and he dug, and he threw out gravel, *ka-ching, ka-ching!* "It's your turn now, Koala," he said.

The koala was resting in the shade, stroking his tail.

"I don't understand how to do it," whined the koala. "Could you show me one more time?"

The kangaroo bent over and he dug, and he dug, and he dug, and he threw out gravel, *ka-ching, ka-ching!* He dug, and he dug, and he dug, and he threw out gravel, *ka-ching, ka-ching!* Then he stood up and said, "Koala, you must take your turn digging."

The koala was combing and stroking his tail. "My tail hurts," he whined. "I think I have a splinter in my tail."

The kangaroo groaned. He bent over and he dug, and he dug, and he dug, and he threw out gravel, *ka-ching, ka-ching!* He dug, and he dug, and he dug, and he threw out gravel, *ka-ching, ka-ching!* "I can smell the water," the kangaroo shouted. "Koala, come dig!"

The koala walked over to the hole. He smelled the water, and he heard the water rushing into the hole. The koala dived in headfirst and began to drink, *shoosh, shoosh, shoosh, shoosh.*

"I hear you drinking," cried the kangaroo. "Get out of the hole, Koala! Let me drink."

The koala kept drinking, *shoosh, shoosh, shoosh, shoosh.*

"I did all the digging!" cried the kangaroo. "I deserve to drink first."

The koala kept drinking, *shoosh, shoosh, shoosh, shoosh.*

"Please let me drink," begged the kangaroo. He was so thirsty.

The koala didn't budge. His head and his body were in the hole; only his long, fluffy tail stuck out. The kangaroo took hold of the koala's tail. He only meant to yank the koala out of the hole, but when he pulled on the tail, it snapped off!

Nowadays, the koala stays up in the branches of the gum tree. He's so sad and ashamed that he lost his beautiful tail. But I think he deserves what he got, don't you? That koala was so lazy!

JABUTI AND JAGUAR GO COURTING
Brazil

In the early days of the world, when all the animals lived together and even married into each other's families, Jabuti the Tortoise took a liking to Miss Lizard. He decided to go to her house and see if she liked him, too. Poor Jabuti! When he got to the Lizards' place, everyone was swooning over Mr. Jaguar.

"Mr. Jaguar is so tall and handsome," said Miss Lizard's mother.

"Mr. Jaguar has such a beautiful coat," said Miss Lizard.

"Yes, yes," said Miss Lizard's father. "Mr. Jaguar would make a fine husband for our daughter."

Jabuti thought quickly. "You are right," he said. "Mr. Jaguar is good-looking, but I'm afraid he will never amount to much. Do you know that I ride him around like a horse?"

"What?" gasped Miss Lizard.

"It's true," said Jabuti. "If you want a husband with brains, you should marry me."

Jabuti went home. He lay on his bed and waited. It wasn't long before Mr. Jaguar came storming up to Jabuti's front door.

"Jabuti, you have been telling lies about me!" snarled Mr. Jaguar. "You told Miss Lizard that you ride me like a horse."

Jabuti answered in a weak little whisper, "Mr. Jaguar, you would never let me ride you like a horse."

"Come with me to Miss Lizard's house," Mr. Jaguar said. "Tell her yourself that you don't ride me like a horse."

Jabuti coughed. "I wish I could," he croaked, "but I am too sick. I will go later, when I get better . . . *if* I get better. Or maybe you could carry me to Miss Lizard's place."

"Get on my back," growled Mr. Jaguar. He crouched down low and waited while Jabuti scooted up and got settled. Mr. Jaguar began to walk toward Miss Lizard's house.

"Ai! Ai! Ai!" Jabuti cried. "Your rib bones are sharp, Mr. Jaguar. They are hurting me. Put me down!"

With his teeth, Mr. Jaguar picked up a big, soft leaf. He gave it to Jabuti and said, "Sit on this, and stop complaining."

Jabuti sat on the soft leaf, and Mr. Jaguar began walking.

"Ai! Ai! Ai!" Jabuti cried. "I am going to fall. Put me down."

Mr. Jaguar took a vine between his teeth and said, "Hold on to this, Jabuti. Hold on to both ends, and stop complaining!"

Jabuti held on to the ends of the vine, and Mr. Jaguar began walking.

"Ai! Ai! Ai!" Jabuti cried.

"What's wrong now?" groaned Mr. Jaguar.

"Flies! Mosquitoes! They are getting in my eyes! They are biting me! Take me home, Mr. Jaguar. Take me home right now."

Mr. Jaguar snapped off a long, thin branch with his teeth and gave it to Jabuti, saying, "Hit them with this, Jabuti, and stop complaining."

Jabuti held the twig in his mouth and he swung it around. He hit Mr. Jaguar, but Mr. Jaguar didn't notice because he was running as fast as he could to Miss Lizard's house.

Mr. Lizard was lounging on a tree trunk. He saw Mr. Jaguar galloping along, and he began to shout, "Everyone, come and see. It's true! It's true! Yes, Jabuti *does* ride Mr. Jaguar like a horse!"

Mr. Jaguar was running so fast and panting so hard, he didn't hear the shouting and laughing. He stopped in front of the Lizards' house and said, "Tell them, Jabuti. Tell them it isn't true. Tell them you don't ride me like a horse."

"Miss Lizard," said Jabuti, "will you marry me? We can ride to church on my horse."

Jabuti slid to the ground, and not a moment too soon. His horse bolted and headed for the deepest part of the jungle. Miss Lizard and her family decided that Jabuti the Tortoise would make a much more suitable husband than Mr. Saddle-Horse Jaguar.

WHY DO MONKEYS LIVE IN TREES?
Ghana

Long ago, the monkey and the leopard were friends, but their friendship ended. It happened like this. One day, the leopard lay across the branch of a tree, trying to fall asleep, but she couldn't, because so many fleas were biting her.

"Please, my dear friend," she said to the monkey, "catch these fleas that are bothering me." The monkey sat beside the leopard and caught the fleas. Slowly, the leopard's eyes closed. A smile spread across her face. She began to snore.

"The leopard looks so peaceful," the monkey chuckled. "I can't help myself. I *must* tie her tail to this tree." He knotted her tail around a small branch. Then he climbed up to the very top of the tree.

After a short nap, the leopard yawned and stood up. Her tail pulled her back down. She looked around and saw that her tail was tied to the tree. Then she heard the monkey laughing, up above her.

"Come down here and untie my tail," the leopard growled.

"Oh, no," the monkey answered. "You might catch me and eat me."

The leopard pleaded with every animal she saw. Only the snail agreed to help. The snail took the end of the leopard's tail in her mouth, and verrrrry slowly she untied the leopard's tail. It took her two whole days! The leopard spent every moment of those two days planning a way to get even with the monkey.

The leopard visited all her friends and relatives and told them what the monkey had done. "Give a funeral for me, yes, a big funeral with music and dancing," she said. "I will lie down and pretend to be dead, and when the monkey comes to dance at my funeral, I will grab him and eat him."

The leopard stretched out on the ground, and the funeral began. The drummers drummed, and the other animals danced in a circle around the leopard, singing,

"The leopard is dead,
Yes, the leopard is dead.
Come dance! Come dance!
The leopard is dead."

The monkey heard the drums. He wanted to dance, but he stayed safe in the treetop. On the second day of the funeral, the animals danced to the drums and sang,

"The leopard is dead,
Yes, the leopard is dead.
Come dance! Come dance!
The leopard is dead."

The monkey danced across the branches of the tree, but he did not come down. On the third day of the funeral, the monkey heard the song,

"The leopard is dead,
Yes, the leopard is dead.
Come dance! Come dance!
The leopard is dead."

"I can't help myself," said the monkey. He danced down the tree and over to the circle of animals, right up to the place where the leopard lay. Her eyes were open just a bit. She watched the monkey dance closer and closer. Then the leopard JUMPED, and the monkey JUMPED, and the leopard RAN, and the monkey RAN, faster, FASTER, FASTER!

That monkey! He was quicker than the leopard. He climbed to the top of the tallest tree he could find. He's still up there, so afraid that the leopard will catch him. Some days, though, when he's feeling sassy, the monkey hangs from a branch by his tail and calls down to the leopard, "Help me! Help me! My tail is tied to the tree. Please come up and untie it for me." The leopard just snarls, rrrrrrr. And now you know why monkeys live in trees.

JUAN BOBO
Argentina

Once upon a time, a woman had an only son named Juan, and everyone called the boy Juan Bobo—Silly Juan—because he could never do anything right.

One day, Juan Bobo's mother gave him a big cloth sack and sent him to town to buy salt.

Juan Bobo walked to town and bought the salt. He put the salt in the sack and swung the sack over his shoulder.

Oof! The sack was heavy. It hurt Juan Bobo's back. He put it down on the ground and dragged it behind him. "That's much better," Juan Bobo said. He walked until he came to the river, and he crossed the river as he always did, stepping from rock to rock, and he dragged the sack behind him in the water.

"The sack is much lighter now," said Juan Bobo after he had crossed the river.

"Here is the salt, Mama," said Juan, and he dropped the wet, empty sack on the kitchen table.

"Juan, what a *bobo* you are!" she said. "You should have carried it in a wagon."

The next day, Juan Bobo's mother sent him to borrow a needle from his godmother. Juan Bobo got his little wagon and pulled it down the road to his godmother's house. But when he got back home, he couldn't find the needle anywhere.

"I think it bounced off the wagon," he said.

"People are right to call you a *bobo*," sighed Juan Bobo's mother. "Everyone knows you should have stuck it in your hat."

The next day, Juan Bobo's mother asked him to go to town and buy a pound of butter. Juan Bobo bought the pound of butter. He took off his hat, put the butter inside, and put it back on his head.

What a hot day it was! The sun beat down on Juan Bobo. The sun beat down on Juan Bobo's hat. When Juan Bobo got home, his hat and his hair and his face were dripping with melted butter.

"Oh, Juan!" cried his mother. "What am I going to do with you? Even a *bobo* knows that you should have put it in a box with cool leaves."

The next day, Juan Bobo's mother sent him to borrow a shovel from his godfather. Juan Bobo got a box and filled it with cool leaves. But the shovel would not fit inside the box. So Juan Bobo borrowed his godfather's saw, and he sawed the handle of the shovel into little pieces.

"Now it fits in the box!" said Juan, and he hurried home.

"Oh, no," blubbered Juan Bobo's mother. "Why did you cut the shovel to pieces? Don't you know that you should have carried it on your shoulder?"

The sun set. The sun rose. Juan Bobo's mother said, "Last week I loaned our cow to your uncle. Please go and get it back."

Juan Bobo ran to his uncle's house. It took Juan Bobo a long time to get the cow onto his shoulder. Very slowly, Juan walked home. The cow was not happy at all, and mooed loudly. Juan staggered along, past the king's palace. On the balcony of the palace sat the king's daughter, who was known as "The Princess Who Never Laughs," for she was always sad. The king had promised that he would give half his kingdom to the person who could cheer her up.

On that particular morning, the princess was crying her eyes out when along came Juan Bobo carrying a cow on his shoulder. The princess heard the cow's loud moo, and she glanced up. What a sight! She began to giggle. Juan Bobo began to giggle. The princess began to laugh. Juan Bobo began to laugh.

The king kept his promise. He gave half his kingdom to Juan Bobo. Not long afterward, the princess and Juan were married, and no one ever called him Juan Bobo again. They called him "Your Highness."

Zapatito roto,	Little broken shoe,
Y usted me cuenta otro.	The next tale comes from *you.*

THE WONDERFUL PANCAKE
Ireland

Once upon a time, when pigs were swine and birds made their nests in old men's beards, a cat and a mouse and a little red hen lived together in a tiny house. One day, the little red hen said, "Let's bake a pancake and have a feast."

"Oh, yes, let's!" said the cat, and "Oh, yes, let's!" said the mouse.

"Who will grind the wheat into flour?" asked the hen.

"I won't," said the cat, and "I won't," said the mouse.

"I will grind it myself," said the little red hen, and so she did.

"Who will make the pancake?" asked the little red hen.

"I won't," said the cat, and "I won't," said the mouse.

"I will make it myself," said the little red hen, and so she did.

"Who will eat the pancake?" asked the little red hen.

"I will," said the cat, and "I will," said the mouse.

"No you won't," said the hen. "I will eat it all myself."

Then the pancake jumped up and said, "First you'll have to catch me!" It rolled out the door, and after it ran the mouse and the cat and the little red hen.

The pancake rolled along, and it passed by a barn full of threshers. "Where are you going, little pancake?" they asked.

"I jumped from the pan
And away I ran
From the mouse and the cat,
    And the little red hen,
        And I'll run away from you if I can!"

The threshers chased after the pancake with their flails flailing, but the pancake rolled faster, and it came to a ditch full of diggers. "Where are you going, little pancake?" they asked.

"I jumped from the pan
And away I ran
From the mouse and the cat,
And the little red hen,
And a barn full of threshers,
And I'll run away from you if I can!"

All the ditchdiggers ran after the pancake, shaking their shovels in the air, but the pancake rolled faster and came to a well full of washers. "Where are you going, little pancake?" they asked.

"I jumped from the pan
And away I ran
From the mouse and the cat,
And the little red hen,
And a barn full of threshers,
And a ditch full of diggers,
And I'll run away from you if I can!"

All the washers chased after the pancake, waving their wet wash in the air, but the little pancake rolled faster, and at last it came to a stream where it met a fox, and the fox asked where it was going.

"I jumped from the pan
And away I ran
From the mouse and the cat,
And the little red hen,
And a barn full of threshers,
And a ditch full of diggers,
And a well full of washers,
And I'll run away from you, too, if I can!"

"But you can't swim, little pancake," said the fox, "and if you try, you'll end up nothing but crumbs."

"Will you carry me across?" asked the pancake.

"What'll you give me if I do?" asked the fox.

"A kiss at Christmas and an egg at Easter."

"Very well," said the fox. "Up you go." He sat on his haunches with his nose in the air. The pancake rolled up the fox's tail and along the fox's back and sat between the fox's ears.

"That's not high enough," said the fox. "Sit on the tip of my nose now."

The pancake rolled to the tip of the fox's nose, and that sly fox tossed the pancake up in the air, and caught it in his mouth, and sent it down the red lane, and that was the end of one little pancake.

ᛕURATKO THE TERRIBLE
Czech Republic

Once there lived an old woman and an old man, and they had no children. "If only we had a child or a chick of our own," they used to say. "How we would spoil it!"

One day, the hen in the barnyard hatched an egg. The old man and the old woman were delighted. They named the chick Kuratko and they petted him and pampered him like a baby. Kuratko grew and grew. What an enormous appetite he had! *"Cock-a-doodle-doo!"* he crowed at all hours of the day and night. "I'm hungry! Give me something to eat!"

"We mustn't feed that chick so much," Grandma grumbled. "He's eating us out of house and home." But Grandpa wouldn't listen. He fed the chick and fed the chick some more, until there was no food left for him or Grandma.

Grandma sat spinning at her spinning wheel, trying to forget how hungry she was, and Grandpa sat in his rocking chair, chewing on the ends of his mustache. Kuratko strutted into the room, flapped his wings, and crowed, "*Cock-a-doodle-doo!* I'm hungry! Give me something to eat!"

"I will never feed you again!" Grandma shouted.

"*Cock-a-doodle-doo*, I'll just eat you!" Kuratko opened his beak and in went Grandma, spinning wheel and all.

"Oh, Kuratko!" Grandpa cried. "What have you done with Grandma?"

"I ate Grandma, spinning wheel and all, and *cock-a-doodle-doo*, I'll just eat you!" He opened his beak and swallowed Grandpa, rocking chair and all.

Then Kuratko the Terrible strutted down the road, crowing merrily. He met a policeman on his bicycle. "Good gracious, Kuratko!" the policeman declared. "What a great big belly you've got!"

"My belly should be big," said Kuratko. "I have just eaten Grandma, spinning wheel and all, and Grandpa, rocking chair and all, and *cock-a-doodle-doo*, I'll just eat you!"

Before the policeman knew what was happening, Kuratko opened his beak and swallowed him, bicycle and all! Then that terrible chick strutted on down the road, crowing merrily.

Soon he met the princess, riding on her pony. "Good gracious, Kuratko," said the princess. "What a great big belly you've got!"

"My belly should be big," said Kuratko, "for haven't I just eaten Grandma, spinning wheel and all, and Grandpa, rocking chair and all, and the policeman, bicycle and all? *Cock-a-doodle-doo*, I'll just eat you!"

Kuratko opened his beak and swallowed the princess, pony and all! Then that terrible chick strutted down the road, crowing merrily.

Soon he met Kotsor the Big Black Cat. Kotsor blinked his eyes in astonishment. "Good gracious, Kuratko, what a great big belly you've got!"

"I should think my belly was big," said Kuratko, "for haven't I just eaten Grandma, spinning wheel and all, and Grandpa, rocking chair and all, and the policeman, bicycle and all, and the princess, pony and all? *Cock-a-doodle-doo*, I'll just eat you!"

Kuratko opened his beak and swallowed Kotsor the Big Black Cat. Down went the cat into the dark belly of Kuratko. He unsheathed his claws and began to tear and scratch his way out. At that, Kuratko the Terrible toppled over and crowed one last time, "*Cock-a-doodle-doooooo!*"

Then Kotsor the Big Black Cat jumped out of Kuratko's belly, and after him came the princess on her pony, and the policeman on his bicycle, and Grandpa, dragging his rocking chair, and Grandma, carrying her spinning wheel, and they all hurried home. Kotsor the Big Black Cat followed Grandma and Grandpa to their house and begged them to give him Kuratko for his dinner.

"You may have him, for all I care," Grandma said. "He was an ungrateful chick and I never want to hear his name again."

So Kotsor the Big Black Cat had a wonderful dinner. To this day, when he remembers it, he licks his lips, and combs his whiskers, and purrs, and purrs, and purrs.

Too MANY FISH
Borneo

Once the mouse deer went fishing with the flying fox, the tortoise, and the porcupine. From vines they wove a net. They spread the net across the waves and waited. When they pulled the net ashore, it was filled with flashing, flipping fish.

"What a lot of fish!" said the flying fox.

"We'll never be able to eat them all," said the tortoise.

The porcupine sighed, "They're sure to spoil."

"Not if we dry them," said the mouse deer.

They hung the fish to dry in the hot sun and went inside their house for a nap.

A fishy aroma arose on the breeze and floated into the forest, where Gergasi the Giant smelled it. *Kertak, kertak, kertak!* Trees snapped as Gergasi lumbered along, looking for the fish. When he found them, he swallowed them all without chewing once. Then he knocked on the door of the little house. "I'm still hungry!" he growled. "Is anyone home?"

The mouse deer was frightened. "No," he shouted, and his voice echoed loudly off the walls.

"You have a big voice," said Gergasi. "Who are you?"

"I'm a giant!" declared the mouse deer, surprising even himself.

"A giant? Come out where I can see you!"

"No, I am resting. But I will show you one of my ears." The mouse deer nudged the flying fox, and the flying fox spread his leathery wing out the window.

"Your ear is big," Gergasi said, grinning, "but *mine* are bigger."

"Look at my sharp whiskers!" the mouse deer bragged as the porcupine poked his long quills out the door.

"Your whiskers are sharp, but *mine* are sharper."

"Ouch! Ouch!" cried the mouse deer. "A flea is biting me!" The mouse deer and the flying fox and the porcupine lifted the tortoise to the window. Gergasi gazed at it.

"That's a fat flea," Gergasi grimaced, "but *mine* are fatter. Come out now!"

"What shall we do?" the porcupine pleaded.

"Tie me with vines," whispered the mouse deer, and he told them his plan.

"Waah!" the mouse deer wailed as he rolled down the ladder to the ground.

Gergasi looked at him. "So, little mouse deer! Were you pretending to be a giant? You didn't fool me."

"Waah!" cried the mouse deer again.

"What's the matter with you? Why are you all tied up with vines?" the monster asked.

"This is the only cure."

"The only cure for what?"

"The horrible sickness."

"What horrible sickness?"

"The horrible sickness that comes from eating too many fish."

Gergasi patted his bulging belly. "Too many fish?"

"First you eat too many fish," the mouse deer explained. "A little while later, your toes tingle, and your knees knock, and your stomach sloshes, and your nose goes numb, and then, unless someone ties you up . . ."

"Unless someone ties you up . . . what?" demanded Gergasi.

"It's too terrible to even talk about," murmured the mouse deer.

"My toes are tingling!" Gergasi gasped. *Knock, knock, knock,* went his

knees. "I think I hear my stomach sloshing. Do you hear my stomach sloshing?"

The mouse deer listened. "Yes," he said helpfully.

Gergasi pinched his nose. "My nose is numb. Hurry! Tie me up right now!"

"I will," declared the mouse deer, "if you lie down and close your eyes."

Gergasi stretched out on the sandy beach. He squinched his eyes shut. "Waah!" he wailed.

The flying fox and the porcupine and the tortoise tied Gergasi with vines from head to foot. They rolled him into the water and watched him float away on the waves, still wailing, "Waah!" Since that day, Gergasi the Giant has never been seen on the island of Borneo.

THE TORTOISE AND THE IROKO MAN
Nigeria

Alo o! Alo o! A story! A story!

There was a drought in the land. The crops shriveled and died. People and animals were starving. Only the Iroko Man was fat, because his garden was full of yams.

The tortoise was so thin, you could hear his bones rattle in his shell. He went to see the Iroko Man, begging, "Please, give me just one yam."

"Here is a yam," said the Iroko Man. "Cook it. Eat it. Tonight I will come to your house and hit you one time with my hard, hard iroko wood club. One yam, one hit."

The tortoise took the yam and walked home. On the way, he met a goat.

"Would you share that yam with me?" the goat asked.

"I'd be delighted," said the tortoise. They went to his house and cooked the yam and ate it.

"Why don't you spend the night?" the tortoise asked. "You can sleep beside the door. By the way, I am expecting a delivery tonight. When you hear a knock, open the door and say, 'Let me have it.'"

In the dark of night, the goat heard a knock. He opened the door. "Let me have it," he said. The Iroko Man hit the goat on the head with his iroko club, but the club struck the goat's hard horns and he didn't feel a thing.

"This tortoise is strong," thought the Iroko Man. "He doesn't even make a noise when I hit him."

56

The next day, the tortoise went to see the Iroko Man again. This time he asked for two yams.

"You may have two yams," said the Iroko Man. "But you know the deal. Two yams, two hits."

The tortoise took two yams, and as he was walking home, he met a warthog.

"Will you share those yams with me?" asked the warthog.

"Gladly," said the tortoise, and he and the warthog went home and cooked and ate the yams.

"Why don't you spend the night," the tortoise asked the warthog. "You can sleep beside the door. By the way, I am expecting a delivery. When you hear a knock, open the door and say, 'Let me have it.'"

After dark, there was a knock at the door. The sleepy warthog opened it and said, "Let me have it."

The Iroko Man thought to himself, "Last time I hit the tortoise from the top. This time I will hit him from the side." He swung sideways. His club hit the warthog's sharp tusk, but the warthog didn't even feel it.

"This tortoise is very strong," the Iroko Man grumbled.

The next day, the tortoise went to the Iroko Man and asked for seven yams.

"You know what that means, don't you?"

"Yes," said the tortoise. "Seven yams, seven hits."

On his way home, the tortoise met a civet cat.

"Will you share those yams?" asked the cat.

"Yes, indeed," said the tortoise. He and the civet cat cooked the yams and ate them.

"Why don't you spend the night," said the tortoise. "You can sleep beside the door. By the way, I am expecting a delivery. When you hear a knock, open the door and say, 'Let me have it.'"

Now, civet cats are heavy sleepers. When the Iroko Man came knocking, the civet cat didn't wake up. "Hey, Civet Cat, wake up!" the tortoise whispered. The civet cat kept on sleeping. The Iroko Man knocked again, louder.

The civet cat kept on sleeping. The tortoise shouted, "Hey, Civet Cat, open the door!"

Then the Iroko Man understood that the tortoise had made other animals take the hits for him. He pushed the door open and went inside the house. The tortoise pulled all his soft parts into his shell and closed up tight. The Iroko Man felt all around and found the tortoise, and hit him seven times.

Ever since that night, the tortoise's shell has cracks where the iroko club hit his back. Don't be like the tortoise. If you see danger coming, don't try to turn it against someone else. You must work together to avoid danger.

DON'T WAKE KING ALIMANGO
Philippines

A long time ago, when the world was much quieter than it is now, a crab named Alimango lived in a sandy cave by the riverbank and was king of all the small creatures who dwelled nearby.

"I am tired," the king announced one evening. "I am going to sleep, and I do not wish to be disturbed. Anyone who wakes me will be punished!"

The little guard crabs snapped their claws, *pitik, pitik,* and chirped, "Yes, Your Majesty! Yes, Your Majesty!"

Alimango nestled in his sandy bed. Suddenly, some frogs laughed, *batak-tak, batak-tak.* The king rushed to the door of his cave. "Be quiet!" he screeched. "Don't you know I'm trying to sleep?" The frogs laughed again, *batak-tak, batak-tak.*

Alimango scuttled sideways out of his house. "Guards," he cried. "Arrest those frogs at once!"

The guard crabs scurried away, *pitik, pitik,* and pinched the frogs and dragged them before the king.

"So," said King Alimango, "you dare to laugh, *batak-tak, batak-tak,* and wake me up?"

"It wasn't our fault!" croaked the frogs. "We saw someone dragging her house behind her, *dugay, dugay.* We couldn't help laughing."

"Who was dragging a house behind her, *dugay, dugay?*"

"It was the snail."

"Guards! Arrest the snail right now!" the king commanded.

The little crabs scurried off, *pitik*, *pitik*, and found the snail and carried her to the king.

"So," said King Alimango. "You were dragging your house along behind you, *dugay*, *dugay*, and you made the frogs laugh, *batak-tak*, *batak-tak*, and woke me up!"

"It wasn't my fault!" sobbed the snail. "Someone was carrying fire that sparkled, *kislap*, *kislap*. I was afraid he would burn my house down."

"Who was carrying fire that sparkled, *kislap*, *kislap*?" the king demanded.

"The firefly."

"Guards, arrest that firefly," ordered the king.

And the little crabs scurried off, *pitik*, *pitik*, and brought back the firefly.

"So," said the king. "You carried fire that sparkled, *kislap*, *kislap*, and scared the snail so that she dragged her house behind her, *dugay*, *dugay*, and made the frogs laugh, *batak-tak*, *batak-tak*, and woke me up!"

"It wasn't my fault!" the firefly whined. "I had to carry fire because someone was buzzing, *gong-yong*, *gong-yong*, and trying to bite me."

"Who was buzzing, *gong-yong*, *gong-yong*, and trying to bite you?"

"The mosquito," said the firefly.

"Guards! What are you waiting for? Bring the mosquito to me!" the king commanded.

The guard crabs scurried away, *pitik, pitik,* and caught the mosquito and took her to the king.

"So," said Alimango. "You were buzzing, *gong-yong, gong-yong,* and trying to bite the firefly so that he carried fire that sparkled, *kislap, kislap,* and scared the snail so that she dragged her house behind her, *dugay, dugay,* and made the frogs laugh, *batak-tak, batak-tak,* and woke me up!"

"It wazzzn't my fault! It wazzzn't my fault!" buzzed the mosquito. "I have to bite other creatures in order to live. It's my nature."

"So! It *was* your fault!" shrieked King Alimango. "Guards, tie her up and throw her in jail."

But the mosquito slipped out of their claws. She soared high in the air, then dived right at King Alimango. The king disappeared into his cave and filled the doorway with sand.

That mosquito has been chasing King Alimango ever since. But she can't see very well, and she mistakes the holes of people's ears for the entrance to King Alimango's cave. Into our ears, she buzzes, "*Gong-yong, gong-yong!* It wazzzn't my fault! It wazzzn't my fault! It wazzzn't my fault!"

BUGGY WUGGY
Italy

Long ago there was a farm, and on that farm lived many birds. The rooster was their king, and all day long he crowed, "*Kee-kee-ree-kee!* Magnificent me! *Kee-kee-ree-kee!*"

One afternoon, the wind blew a scrap of paper over the barnyard fence. The paper landed at the rooster's feet. He looked down and saw that there was writing on it.

"What does it say?" asked the hen. She didn't know how to read. Neither did the rooster, but he pretended that he did.

"It's a letter from the Pope. He wants me to come to Rome and be king of the entire country."

"May I come with you?" the hen asked.

"Of course," said the rooster, who now believed his own story. "*Kee-kee-ree-kee!* King Rooster Dooster, Queen Henny Wenny."

"*Qua, qua!* May I come, too?" asked the duck.

"Yes," said the rooster. "*Kee-kee-ree-kee!* King Rooster Dooster, Queen Henny Wenny, Duke Ducky Lucky."

"Don't leave without me!" said a tiny voice.

The rooster looked up and down and all around, and on the ground he spied a bug.

"What will *you* do in Rome?" asked the rooster.

"I'll be your general and protect you," boasted the bug.
The rooster crowed, "*Kee-kee-ree-kee!* King Rooster Dooster, Queen Henny
    Wenny, Duke Ducky Lucky, General Buggy Wuggy."

The three birds marched toward Rome with the bug creep-creep-creeping along behind. Just before sunset, they arrived at a grassy meadow.

"Rome is very far away," sighed King Rooster Dooster. "We will spend the night here."

"A queen does not sleep outdoors," sniffed Henny Wenny.

"*Qua!* Let's build houses for ourselves," suggested Duke Ducky Lucky.

So King Rooster Dooster pecked up twigs and made a twig house. Queen Henny Wenny gathered leaves in her beak and built a leafy cottage next door. Duke Ducky Lucky pulled up grass and made a little grass hut. They went inside their houses and fell fast asleep.

Buggy Wuggy shook his head. "Those houses don't look safe to me," he grumbled. "I think I'll dig a hole."

All this time, someone was lurking behind a tree, watching and waiting for them to fall asleep. It was the wolf! He tiptoed to the twig house. *Whoosh!* He blew it down and ate Rooster Dooster in one big bite. He crept to the leafy cottage. *Whoosh!* He blew it down and gobbled Henny Wenny in one gulp. He snuck over to the grass hut. *Whoosh!* He blew it down and swallowed Ducky Lucky in one slurp.

The wolf was so full and so fat he could hardly walk. He waddled to the hole that Buggy Wuggy had made. Into the hole he blew and blew and blew. But the clever bug just dug deeper and deeper, and as he dug he sang, "You can't catch me! You can't catch me!"

"I can, too," the wolf snorted. He took a deep, deep breath and let out such an enormous *whoosh* that he *whooshed* out Rooster Dooster and Henny Wenny and Ducky Lucky (all a bit soggy but none the worse for their troubles, because, as you recall, the wolf had swallowed each of them whole). The birds bustled back to the barnyard, and since that day, none of them has ever let out so much as a peep about Rome. As for Buggy Wuggy, he was so proud and pleased that he had protected them. He kept marching toward Rome, where he was sure he would be made a general. But Buggy Wuggy is so small and Rome is so far away, you can probably still see him creep-creep-creeping along that road today.

Rome 2000 km

THE TEENY-TINY CHICK AND THE SNEAKY OLD CAT
Myanmar, formerly Burma

"Please bake me a cake," said the teeny-tiny chick.

"I will," said the hen, "if you bring me bits and pieces of firewood that people throw away."

The chick went to the kitchen of the house next door, but as she was picking up wood splinters, the sneaky old cat caught her. "Let me go!" peeped the teeny-tiny chick. "I am gathering firewood so that my mother can bake me a cake. If you let me go, I will share it with you."

"All right," meowed the cat, and he spat her out.

The teeny-tiny chick hurried home and told her mother what happened.

"Don't worry, dear," said the hen. "I will bake a cake that is big enough for you *and* that sneaky old cat."

When the cake was baked, the hen said, "Don't forget to leave a piece for the sneaky old cat." But the cake tasted so nice that the teeny-tiny chick ate it all up.

"Uh-oh!" said the chick. "There isn't any left for the sneaky old cat."

"You greedy little thing," scolded the hen.

"Maybe the sneaky old cat forgot," said the chick. "Maybe he won't come. He probably doesn't even know where we live."

"*Meow! Meow!* Where is my cake? If you don't give me my cake, I'll eat you up, you bad little chick, and your mother, too."

The teeny-tiny chick began to run. "Follow me," she called to her mother. They hurried to the house next door and headed for the kitchen. The chick jumped into a big clay pot and the hen jumped in after her.

The sneaky old cat ran into the house. "I saw you come in," he meowed, "and there is only one door. Sooner or later you will come out of your hiding place."

Inside the clay pot, the hen and the chick waited so quietly. But there was flour in the clay pot, and some of it got into the teeny-tiny chick's beak. "Mama, I have to sneeze," she whimpered.

"If you sneeze, the old cat will hear you, and he will catch us and eat us."

"Mama, I need to sneeze just a little bit."

"Do you want to be the cat's dinner?" whispered her mother.

"Please, let me sneeze just a teensy little bit."

"No," said her mother.

"Let me sneeze just a half a teensy little bit."

"No, no, no!" said her mother.

The teeny-tiny little chick just couldn't help herself. She sneezed, "Ah . . . ah . . . ah . . . CHOO!"

BOOM! The clay pot exploded!

That sneaky old cat howled and hissed and yowled and ran away and hid for a week, and he never did catch the teeny-tiny chick.

THE SINGING PUMPKIN
Iran

Yaki boud, yaki na boud. Once there was and once there was not an old woman who lived all alone with her big white dog. Early one morning, the old woman decided to visit her granddaughter, who lived far away, over the mountain.

"Stay here and guard the house," the old woman told her big white dog, and off she went, walking along the path that led up the mountain.

In a cave on the mountainside lived a hungry djinni—an ogre! He heard the old woman's footsteps. He stood in the path, blocking her way.

"Old woman," the djinni roared. "I am going to eat you for my dinner."

"*Tch, tch,*" scolded the old woman. "What sort of dinner would I be for a big djinni like you? Listen. I am on my way to my granddaughter's house, and she is such a good cook, I will eat and grow very fat. You should wait and eat me on my way back."

"That's exactly what I'll do," said the ogre. "Hurry up and get fat, and I will eat you on your way back."

The old woman kept walking until she arrived at her granddaughter's house. Her granddaughter was so happy to see her! She cooked rice and stew and kebabs and cakes and puddings, and the old woman ate and ate. She grew very plump, indeed.

"Oh, dear," the old woman groaned. "I think I am too fat to walk home. But I must go because my big white dog will miss me."

"Don't worry, Nana," said her granddaughter. "There is a great big pumpkin in my garden. If we cut off the top and scoop out the middle, you can get inside. I will put the top back on and push the pumpkin to the top of the mountain. That way, you will be able to roll home."

"Wonderful!" cried the old woman, and she helped her granddaughter cut the top off the pumpkin. Together they hollowed it out, and then the old woman snuggled down inside. The granddaughter popped the top on the pumpkin and pushed it to the top of the mountain. Then she let go.

Oh, the ride in the pumpkin was so much fun! The old woman began to sing,

"Roll, my pumpkin, roll along,
Bumpity, bumpity, bump!"

The djinni saw the pumpkin rolling down the mountain and he thought, "Hmm. Pumpkins do not usually roll past my cave." Then he heard the pumpkin sing,

"Roll, my pumpkin, roll along,
Bumpity, bumpity, bump!"

"Pumpkins do not sing," said the djinni, and he stood in the path, held out his hand, and stopped the rolling pumpkin.

"Come out, old woman!" the djinni ordered.

"I can't," said the old woman.

"Yes, you can," laughed the djinni.

"I can't come out until you say the magic words."

"What magic words?" asked the djinni.

"You must say, 'Come here, my big white dog.'"

"Come here, my big white dog," said the djinni.

"Louder!" said the old woman.

The djinni shouted, "Come here, my big white dog!"

"Louder!" said the old woman.

"Come heeee–"

But the djinni didn't finish saying the magic words, because the big white dog bounded up, barking fiercely, and chased him far away. Then the dog gave the pumpkin a nudge with his nose, and the old woman rolled home, singing,

"Roll, my pumpkin, roll along,
Bumpity, bumpity, bump!"

THE MIGHTY CATERPILLAR
South Africa: Masai

One morning, Enkitejo the Hare left home to look for food. While she was gone, a woolly caterpillar crawled into her house. When Enkitejo returned, she saw the caterpillar's tracks in the dirt outside her door. "Those look like the marks of someone's shoelaces," she said. "Who is in my house?"

The caterpillar answered in a big, loud voice,

"I am a mighty warrior,
Son of the long one."

"What is a warrior doing in my house?" Enkitejo wondered. She hopped off to see Spotted One the Hyena. "There is a mighty warrior in my house," she said. "Please come and help me get him out."

The hyena crouched by the door and growled, "Who is in the house of Enkitejo?"

The caterpillar answered in his big, loud voice,

"I am a mighty warrior,
Son of the long one.
I toss the hyena higher than the trees!"

"Enkitejo, my friend," yipped the hyena, "this is really not my fight. Good-bye."

Enkitejo went to see Club-on-the-Nose the Rhinoceros. "Come reason with the warrior who has taken over my house," she pleaded. The rhinoceros agreed. He went to the door of the house and bellowed, "Who is in the house of Enkitejo?"

The caterpillar answered in his big, loud voice,

> "I am a mighty warrior,
> Son of the long one.
> I toss the hyena higher than the trees,
> I crush the rhinoceros into the dust!"

"*Anga!*" snorted the rhinoceros. "I'd better start running before he crushes *me* into dust!"

Enkitejo went to see Arm-for-a-Nose the Elephant. The elephant came to the door of the house and trumpeted, "Who is in the house of my Enkitejo?"

The caterpillar answered in his big, loud voice,

"I am a mighty warrior,
Son of the long one.
I toss the hyena higher than the trees,
I crush the rhinoceros into the dust,
I squash the elephant flatter than a cow pie!"

"*Anga!*" cried the elephant. "I do not want to be squashed flatter than a cow pie. Good-bye, my friend. I'll see you later."

Enkitejo decided to ask Sees Everything the Frog for help. The frog sat in front of Enkitejo's door. His throat ballooned and his voice boomed,

> "I am the long-tongued leaper,
> I am the crafty creeper,
> I am slippery and slimy,
> I am gruesome, green, and grimy,
> And I am coming to get you!"

From inside the house came a frightened voice, "Ple-e-ease don't hurt me. Ple-e-ease don't hurt me. I'm just a little woolly caterpillar."

Enkitejo and the frog dragged that mighty warrior out into the daylight. How they laughed, *kweni, kweni, kweni*, when they saw that a woolly caterpillar had caused such big trouble.

ONE GOOD TURN DESERVES ANOTHER
Mexico

Hop, stop, sniff. Hop, stop, sniff. A mouse was going across the desert. Suddenly, she heard a voice, "Help! Help me!" The sound came from under a rock. "Pleasssse get me out of here," said the voice, with an unmistakable hiss.

The mouse placed her front paws against the rock. She was small, but she gave it her best. The rock rolled aside and out slid a snake.

"Thank you *sssso* much," said the snake as he curled a coil around the mouse. "I was stuck under that rock for a long time. I am very hungry."

"But you wouldn't eat *me*," squeaked the mouse.

"Why not?" the snake asked.

"Because I moved the rock," said the mouse. "I saved your life."

"So?" hissed the snake.

"So, one good turn deserves another," the mouse said hopefully.

The snake moved his head from side to side. "You are young," he said. "You don't know much about the world. Good is often repaid with evil."

"That's not fair!" cried the mouse.

"Everyone knows I am right," said the snake. "If you find even one creature who agrees with you, I will set you free."

A crow alighted on a nearby bush.

"Uncle," said the snake to the crow, "help us settle an argument. I was trapped under a rock, and this silly mouse set me free. Now she thinks I shouldn't eat her."

"He should be grateful," the mouse insisted.

"Well, now," said the crow. "I've flown high and I've flown low. I've been just about everywhere. This morning, I ate some grasshoppers that were destroying a farmer's crops. Was he grateful? No. He used me for target practice! Good is often repaid with evil." And off he flew.

An armadillo ambled by. "What's all this noise?" she asked.

"Merely a short conversation before dinner," replied the snake. "My young friend moved a rock and set me free. Now she thinks I shouldn't eat her."

"One good turn deserves another," said the mouse.

"Wait a minute," said the armadillo. "Did you know he was a snake before you moved that rock?"

"I guess I did, but . . ."

"A snake is always a snake," the armadillo declared as she waddled away.

"That settles it," said the snake. "Everyone agrees with me."

"Can't we ask just one more creature?" the mouse pleaded.

"I don't think you'll ever understand," groaned the snake.

A coyote trotted up. "Understand what?" he asked.

"The snake was trapped under that rock," the mouse explained.

"Which rock?" asked the coyote.

"Over there. That rock," said the snake.

"Oh," said the coyote. "The mouse was under that rock."

"No, *I* was under that rock!" said the snake.

"A snake under a rock? Impossible," the coyote snorted. "I have never seen such a thing."

The snake slid into the hole where he had been trapped. "I was in this hole," he hissed, "and that rock was on top of me!"

"This rock?" the coyote asked as she lifted her paw and pushed the rock on top of the snake.

"Yesss!" hissed the snake. "Now show him, little mouse! Show him how you set me free."

But the mouse was already far away. "Thank you, cousin," she called as she ran. "I'll return the favor someday."

"Yes, indeed," said the coyote. "One good turn deserves another."

BIBLIOGRAPHY

Abrahams, Roger D. *African Folktales: Traditional Stories of the Black World*. New York: Pantheon Books, 1983.

Aiken, Riley. *Mexican Folktales from the Borderland*. Dallas: Southern Methodist University Press, 1980.

Bascom, William. *African Folktales in the New World*. Bloomington: Indiana University Press, 1992.

Batchelor, Courtenay Malcolm. *Stories and Storytellers of Brazil*. Havana: n.p., 1953.

Briggs, Katharine Mary. *A Dictionary of British Folk-Tales in the English Language*. Bloomington: Indiana University Press, 1970.

Clouston, William Alexander. *The Book of Noodles: Stories of Simpletons: or, Fools and Their Follies*. London: Elliot Stock, 1888.

Crane, Thomas Frederick. *Italian Popular Tales*. Boston: Houghton Mifflin, 1885.

Crowley, Daniel J. *I Could Talk Old-Story Good: Creativity in Bahamian Folklore*. Berkeley: University of California Press, 1966.

Dasgupta, Sayantani, and Shamita Das Dasgupta. *The Demon Slayers and Other Stories: Bengali Folk Tales*. New York: Interlink Books, 1995.

De Huff, Elizabeth Willis. *Taytay's Tales: Collected and Retold Folk Lore of the Pueblo Indians*. New York: Harcourt, Brace and Company, 1922.

Dorson, Richard M. *Folk Legends of Japan*. Rutland, Vt.: C. E. Tuttle, 1961.

Ellis, Alfred Burdon. *The Ewe-Speaking Peoples*. London: Chapman and Hall, 1890.

Evans, Ivor H. N. *Studies in Religion, Folk-Lore and Custom in British North Borneo and the Malay Peninsula*.Cambridge: Cambridge University Press, 1923.

Fansler, Dean S. *Filipino Popular Tales*. New York: American Folklore Society, 1921.

Fillmore, Parker. *The Shoemaker's Apron: A Second Book of Czechoslovak Fairy Tales and Folk Tales*. New York: Harcourt, Brace and Company, 1920.

Gomes, Edwin Herbert. *Seventeen Years Among the Sea Dyaks of Borneo*. London: Seeley & Co., 1911.

Hollis, Alfred Claud. *The Masai: Their Language and Folklore*. Oxford: Clarendon Press, 1905.

Htin Aung, Maung. *Burmese Folk-Tales*. Oxford: Oxford University Press, 1948.

Jacobs, Joseph. *Indian Fairy Tales*. New York: G. P. Putnam's Sons, 1892.

Jagendorf, M. A. *The Merry Men of Gotham*. New York: Vanguard Press, 1950.

Kennedy, Patrick. *Fireside Stories of Ireland*. Dublin: McGlashan and Gill, 1870.

Leach, Maria. *Noodles, Nitwits, and Numskulls*. Cleveland: World Publishing Company, 1961.

MacDonald, Margaret Read, and John Holmes McDowell. *Traditional Storytelling Today: An International Sourcebook*. Chicago: Fitzroy Dearborn, 1999.

Mayer, Fanny Hagin. *Ancient Tales in Modern Japan: An Anthology of Japanese Folk Tales*. Bloomington: Indiana University Press, 1985.

Mehdevi, Anne. *Persian Folk and Fairy Tales*. London: Chatto & Windus, 1966.

Okpewho, Isidore. *The Oral Performance in Africa*. Ibadan, Nigeria: Spectrum Books, 1990.

Parsons, Elsie W. *Folk-Tales of Andros Island, Bahamas*. Memoirs of the American Folklore Society, 1918.

Ransome, Arthur. *Old Peter's Russian Tales*. New York: Frederick A. Stokes, 1917.

Reed, Alexander Wyclif. *Aboriginal Legends: Animal Tales*. Frenchs Forest, Australia: Reed Books Ltd., 1978.

Robe, Stanley. *Mexican Tales and Legends from Los Altos*. Berkeley: University of California Press, 1970.

Seki, Keigo. *Folktales of Japan*. Translated by Robert J. Adams. Chicago: University of Chicago Press, 1963.

Siddiqui, Ashraf, and Marilyn Lerch. *Toontoony Pie and Other Tales from Pakistan*. Cleveland: World, 1961.

Thompson, Stith. *The Folktale*. Berkeley: University of California Press, 1977.

Thompson, Stith, and Warren E. Roberts. *Types of Indic Oral Tales: India, Pakistan, and Ceylon*. Helsinki: Suomalainen Tiedeakatemia, 1960.

Tichy, Jaroslav. *Persian Fairy Tales*. Retold by Jane Carruth. London: Hamlyn, 1970.

Vidal de Battini, Berta Elena. *Cuentos y leyendas populares de la Argentina*. Vol. 9. Buenos Aires: Ediciones Culturales, 1984.

Wheeler, Howard True. *Tales from Jalisco, Mexico*. Philadelphia: American Folklore Society, 1943.

Wilbert, Johannes, and Karin Simoneau, eds. *Folk Literature of the Mataco Indians*. Los Angeles: Latin American Center Publications, University of California, 1982.

ABOUT THE AUTHOR AND ILLUSTRATOR

JUDY SIERRA knew from an early age that she wanted to be a storyteller and as a child begged her parents to buy her a printing press so she could create her own books. She earned a Ph.D. in folklore and mythology studies from UCLA and for many years had a touring puppet theater specializing in traditional shadow puppetry with her husband, Bob Kaminski. Judy Sierra has also taught puppetry and storytelling and has been an artist-in-residence in schools, libraries, and museums, including the Smithsonian Institution. Currently, she devotes most of her time to writing books for young readers, which include *Antarctic Antics, Counting Crocodiles, Monster Goose,* and *Tasty Baby Belly Buttons.* She is the mother of one son and resides in northern California with her husband.

VALERI GORBACHEV immigrated to the United States from Kiev, Ukraine, in 1991 with his wife and two children. Before coming to the U.S., he was a leading illustrator in the former Soviet Union, where he worked on more than forty children's books, many of which he also wrote. His books have been translated into Finnish, German, and Spanish, and he has participated in many exhibitions of children's book illustrations around the world. His recent titles for young readers include *Nicky and the Big, Bad Wolves,* winner of a *Parent's Guide* Children's Media Award, *Nicky and the Fantastic Birthday Gift, Where Is the Apple Pie?,* and *Chicken Chickens.* Valeri Gorbachev lives with his family in Brooklyn, New York.